Hello, Dinger!

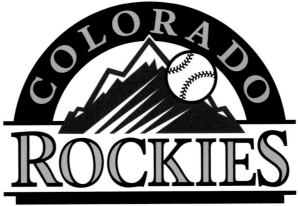

Aimee Aryal

Illustrated by Justin Hilton with D. Moore

www.mascotbooks.com

It was a beautiful day in Denver, Colorado.
Dinger, the Rockies mascot, was on his way
to Coors Field for a baseball game.

As Dinger walked through LoDo, Rockies
fans cheered, "Hello, Dinger!"

Dinger walked down Blake Street to Coors Field-
home of the Colorado Rockies.

In front of the ballpark, Dinger ran into lots of
Rockies fans. They cheered, "Hello, Dinger!"

Dinger arrived on the field just in time
for batting practice. Each player took
practice swings.

As the team's best hitter stepped
to home plate, he said, "Hello, Dinger!"

After batting practice, the Coors Field
grounds crew proudly prepared
the field for play.

As the grounds crew worked,
they cheered, "Hello, Dinger!"

Dinger was feeling hungry. He grabbed a few snacks and a Rockies pennant at the concession stand.

As he made his way back to the field,
a family cheered, "Hello, Dinger!"

Each Rockies player stood on the first base line as the home team was introduced.

Dinger received the largest applause!
Fans cheered, "Hello, Dinger!"

"Play Ball!" yelled the umpire, and the Rockies pitcher delivered a fastball to start the game. "Strike One!" called the umpire.

The umpire noticed Dinger nearby
and said, "Hello, Dinger!"

Dinger went into the bleachers to visit his fans. Everyone was excited to see Dinger.

A family waved and cheered,
"Hello, Dinger!"

It was now time for the seventh inning stretch. Dinger led the crowd as everyone sang "Take Me Out To The Ballgame™!"

Young Rockies fans danced on the dugout with Dinger. They cheered, "Hello, Dinger!"

In the bottom of the ninth inning, a Rockies player hit a game-winning home run over the right field fence.

The team gathered at home
plate to celebrate the victory. The
players cheered, "Rockies win,
Dinger! Rockies win!"

After the game, Dinger was tired. It had been a long day at Coors Field. Dinger walked home and went straight to bed.

Good night, Dinger!

For Anna and Maya ~ Aimee Aryal

For my wife Patricia. Thank you for all of
your love and support. ~ Justin Hilton

For more information about our products,
please visit us online at www.mascotbooks.com.

Mascot Books, Inc.
P.O. Box 220157
Chantilly, VA 20153-0157

Major League Baseball trademarks and copyrights are used
with permission of Major League Baseball Properties, Inc.

ISBN: 1-932888-66-7
Printed in the United States.

www.mascotbooks.com

Title List

Team	Book Title	Author	Team	Book Title	Author
Baseball			**Pro Football**		
Boston Red Sox	Hello, Wally!	Jerry Remy	Carolina Panthers	Let's Go, Panthers!	Aimee Aryal
Boston Red Sox	Wally And His Journey Through Red Sox Nation!	Jerry Remy	Dallas Cowboys	How 'Bout Them Cowboys!	Aimee Aryal
Colorado Rockies	Hello, Dinger!	Aimee Aryal	Green Bay Packers	Go, Pack, Go!	Aimee Aryal
New York Yankees	Let's Go, Yankees!	Yogi Berra	Kansas City Chiefs	Let's Go, Chiefs!	Aimee Aryal
New York Mets	Hello, Mr. Met!	Rusty Staub	Minnesota Vikings	Let's Go, Vikings!	Aimee Aryal
St. Louis Cardinals	Hello, Fredbird!	Ozzie Smith	New York Giants	Let's Go, Giants!	Aimee Aryal
Philadelphia Phillies	Hello, Phillie Phanatic!	Aimee Aryal	New England Patriots	Let's Go, Patriots!	Aimee Aryal
Chicago Cubs	Let's Go, Cubs!	Aimee Aryal	Seattle Seahawks	Let's Go, Seahawks!	Aimee Aryal
Chicago White Sox	Let's Go, White Sox!	Aimee Aryal	Washington Redskins	Hail To The Redskins!	Aimee Aryal
Cleveland Indians	Hello, Slider!	Bob Feller			
			Coloring Book		
			Dallas Cowboys	How 'Bout Them Cowboys!	Aimee Aryal
College					
Alabama	Hello, Big Al!	Aimee Aryal	Maryland	Hello, Testudo!	Aimee Aryal
Alabama	Roll Tide!	Ken Stabler	Michigan	Let's Go, Blue!	Aimee Aryal
Arizona	Hello, Wilbur!	Lute Olson	Michigan State	Hello, Sparty!	Aimee Aryal
Arkansas	Hello, Big Red!	Aimee Aryal	Minnesota	Hello, Goldy!	Aimee Aryal
Auburn	Hello, Aubie!	Aimee Aryal	Mississippi	Hello, Colonel Rebel!	Aimee Aryal
Auburn	War Eagle!	Pat Dye	Mississippi State	Hello, Bully!	Aimee Aryal
Boston College	Hello, Baldwin!	Aimee Aryal	Missouri	Hello, Truman!	Todd Donoho
Brigham Young	Hello, Cosmo!	LaVell Edwards	Nebraska	Hello, Herbie Husker!	Aimee Aryal
Clemson	Hello, Tiger!	Aimee Aryal	North Carolina	Hello, Rameses!	Aimee Aryal
Colorado	Hello, Ralphie!	Aimee Aryal	North Carolina St.	Hello, Mr. Wuf!	Aimee Aryal
Connecticut	Hello, Jonathan!	Aimee Aryal	Notre Dame	Let's Go, Irish!	Aimee Aryal
Duke	Hello, Blue Devil!	Aimee Aryal	Ohio State	Hello, Brutus!	Aimee Aryal
Florida	Hello, Albert!	Aimee Aryal	Ohio State	Brutus' Journey	Aimee Aryal
Florida State	Let's Go, 'Noles!	Aimee Aryal	Oklahoma	Let's Go, Sooners!	Aimee Aryal
Georgia	Hello, Hairy Dawg!	Aimee Aryal	Oklahoma State	Hello, Pistol Pete!	Aimee Aryal
Georgia	How 'Bout Them Dawgs!	Vince Dooley	Penn State	Hello, Nittany Lion!	Aimee Aryal
Georgia Tech	Hello, Buzz!	Aimee Aryal	Penn State	We Are Penn State!	Joe Paterno
Gonzaga	Spike, The Gonzaga Bulldog	Mike Pringle	Purdue	Hello, Purdue Pete!	Aimee Aryal
			Rutgers	Hello, Scarlet Knight!	Aimee Aryal
Illinois	Let's Go, Illini!	Aimee Aryal	South Carolina	Hello, Cocky!	Aimee Aryal
Indiana	Let's Go, Hoosiers!	Aimee Aryal	So. California	Hello, Tommy Trojan!	Aimee Aryal
Iowa	Hello, Herky!	Aimee Aryal	Syracuse	Hello, Otto!	Aimee Aryal
Iowa State	Hello, Cy!	Amy DeLashmutt	Tennessee	Hello, Smokey!	Aimee Aryal
James Madison	Hello, Duke Dog!	Aimee Aryal	Texas	Hello, Hook 'Em!	Aimee Aryal
Kansas	Hello, Big Jay!	Aimee Aryal	Texas A & M	Howdy, Reveille!	Aimee Aryal
Kansas State	Hello, Willie!	Dan Walter	UCLA	Hello, Joe Bruin!	Aimee Aryal
Kentucky	Hello, Wildcat!	Aimee Aryal	Virginia	Hello, CavMan!	Aimee Aryal
Louisiana State	Hello, Mike!	Aimee Aryal	Virginia Tech	Hello, Hokie Bird!	Aimee Aryal
			Virginia Tech	Yea, It's Hokie Game Day!	Frank Beamer
			Wake Forest	Hello, Demon Deacon!	Aimee Aryal
			West Virginia	Hello, Mountaineer!	Aimee Aryal
			Wisconsin	Hello, Bucky!	Aimee Aryal
NBA					
Dallas Mavericks	Let's Go, Mavs!	Mark Cuban			
Kentucky Derby					
Kentucky Derby	White Diamond Runs For The Roses	Aimee Aryal			

More great titles coming soon!

info@mascotbooks.com